I'm Going To R

$5.—

These levels are meant only as guides;
you and your child can best choose a book that's right.

UP TO 50 WORDS

Level 1: Kindergarten–Grade 1 . . . Ages 4–6
- word bank to highlight new words
- consistent placement of text to promote readability
- easy words and phrases
- simple sentences build to make simple stories
- art and design help new readers decode text

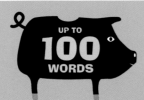
UP TO 100 WORDS

Level 2: Grade 1 . . . Ages 6–7
- word bank to highlight new words
- rhyming texts introduced
- more difficult words, but vocabulary is still limited
- longer sentences and longer stories
- designed for easy readability

UP TO 200 WORDS

Level 3: Grade 2 . . . Ages 7–8
- richer vocabulary of up to 200 different words
- varied sentence structure
- high-interest stories with longer plots
- designed to promote independent reading

MORE THAN 300 WORDS

Level 4: Grades 3 and up . . . Ages 8 and up
- richer vocabulary of more than 300 different words
- short chapters, multiple stories, or poems
- more complex plots for the newly independent reader
- emphasis on reading for meaning

LEVEL 2

Library of Congress Cataloging-in-Publication Data Available

2 4 6 8 10 9 7 5 3 1

Published by Sterling Publishing Co., Inc.
387 Park Avenue South, New York, NY 10016
Text © 2006 by Harriet Ziefert Inc.
Illustrations © 2006 by Pete Whitehead
Distributed in Canada by Sterling Publishing
c/o Canadian Manda Group, 165 Dufferin Street,
Toronto, Ontario, Canada M6K 3H6
Distributed in the United Kingdom by GMC Distribution Services,
Castle Place, 166 High Street, Lewes, East Sussex, England BN7 1XU
Distributed in Australia by Capricorn Link (Australia) Pty. Ltd.
P.O. Box 704, Windsor, NSW 2756, Australia

I'm Going To Read is a trademark of Sterling Publishing Co., Inc.

Printed in China

Sterling ISBN-13: 978-1-4027-3422-9
ISBN-10: 1-4027-3422-0

For information about custom editions, special sales, premium and
corporate purchases, please contact Sterling Special Sales
Department at 800-805-5489 or specialsales@sterlingpub.com.

Be Fair, Share!

Pictures by Pete Whitehead

Sterling Publishing Co., Inc.
New York

Ink, Wink, and Blink
went to the park for a picnic.

"I have a pickle and grapes," said Blink.
"Ink, what do you have?"

"I have a banana," said Ink.
"And I'm sick of bananas!"

"I like bananas," said Blink.

"Let's trade."

Ink gave Blink the banana.
Blink gave Ink the pickle.

"What do you have?"
Blink asked Wink.

"I have a peanut butter
sandwich," said Wink. "I'm sick
of peanut butter!"

"I like peanut butter," said Blink.
"Let's trade."

Wink gave Blink the sandwich.
Blink gave Wink the grapes.

"What do you have?" Wink asked.

"I have a banana and I have a peanut butter sandwich," said Blink.

"But you have two things!" said Ink
and Wink. "It's not fair!"

"I'll be fair!"
said Blink.
"I'll share!"

Blink shared
the banana.
Blink shared
the sandwich.

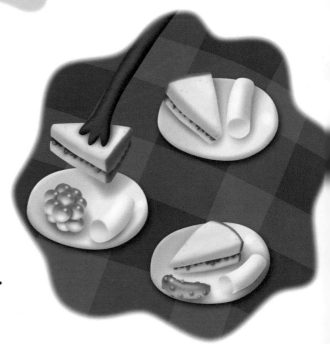

"Now you have more than me!"
Blink said to Ink and Wink.
"You each have three things!"

Ink ate the pickle
and the sandwich—
but not the banana!

"Remember,"
he said,
"I'm sick
of bananas!"

ate   he

Wink ate
the grapes and
the banana—
but not the
sandwich.

"Remember,"
he said, "I'm sick
of peanut butter!"

Blink put her banana on top of the
peanut butter in the sandwich.
She ate it all up. "Yummy!"

"Yuck!" said Ink.
"Yuck!" said Wink.

"You wanted my food,"
said Blink.
"So eat it!"

"I won't!" said Ink.
"I won't eat banana!"

"I won't!" said Wink.
"I won't eat peanut butter."

"Listen up!"
said Blink.

"Ink trade with Wink.
Wink trade with Ink."

"You're bossy, Blink!" said Ink. But he ate the sandwich.

"Blink, you're mean!"
said Wink. But he ate
the banana.

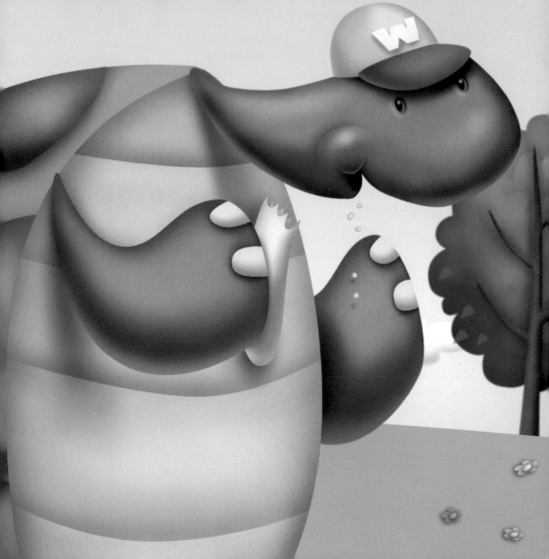

"Now let's play baseball," said Blink.

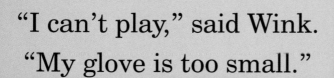

"I can't play," said Wink. "My glove is too small."

"And I can't play," said Ink.
"My glove is too big."

Wink looked at Ink.
Ink looked at Wink.

"Let's trade!" said Ink.

"Okay! Play ball!"
said Blink.